The Cam Jansen Series

★

DON'T FORGET ABOUT THE YOUNG CAM JANSEN
SERIES FOR YOUNGER READERS!

and the Graduation Day Mystery

David A. Adler

illustrated by
Joy Allen

SCHOLASTIC INC.

ISBN 978-0-545-62078-9

12 11 10 9 8 7 6 5 4 3 2 1   13 14 15 16 17 18/0

Printed in the U.S.A.   40

First Scholastic printing, June 2013

Set in New Baskerville

and the
Graduation Day
Mystery

Chapter One

"I'm so proud of Ben," Mrs. Shelton said.

"Me, too," Eric Shelton told his mother. "I'm very proud of Dad."

Grandpa Shelton, Mrs. Shelton, Eric and his twin sisters Donna and Diane, and Cam Jansen were sitting on folding chairs. Eric's baby brother Howie was there, too. He was sleeping on his mother's lap. They were in a large open area in the middle of a college campus. A few thousand other people were there, too.

"Are you sure Dad's here?" Donna asked. "I don't see him."

"I know he's here," Grandpa Shelton said. "I drove him here early this morning."

"He wouldn't miss his own graduation," Mrs. Shelton said.

"And he wouldn't want to miss going to a restaurant to celebrate with us afterward," Grandpa Shelton said.

"Hey, what's taking so long?" a small boy sitting behind the Sheltons asked. "I'm hungry. I want something fun to do."

"Oh, Harry," his mother said. "Eat some animal crackers. Play with your toys."

The boy took some crackers and a toy train from a small shopping bag. He sat on the ground.

"*Choo! Choo!*" he said as he pulled the train through the grass.

"Eric's father has dreamed of this day for a long time," Grandpa Shelton told Cam.

He spoke softly. He didn't want to wake Howie.

"Right after he graduated from high school, he joined the army."

"That's where we met," Mrs. Shelton said. "I was also in the army."

She closed her eyes and smiled. "Ben looked so handsome in his uniform. We got married as soon as we were discharged from the army. Then Ben got a job. He never had time for college."

"Me, too," Eric's sister Diane said. "I don't have time for college. I don't even have time for third grade. After second grade I'm getting a job. I'll bake cookies and sell them."

"Oh, no, you won't," her mother told her. "You're staying in school."

Harry pulled his train through the grass and said, *Choo! Choo!* Then he stopped his train and called out, "All aboard!"

"Your father had to make time for college," Grandpa Shelton whispered to Diane. "He went at night, after work."

"I don't see him anywhere," Donna said. "I think we're at the wrong graduation."

"He's sitting in front," Mrs. Shelton told Donna. "He's wearing a black cap and gown."

"Mom!" Donna said, and pointed ahead. "Millions of people up there are wearing black caps and gowns!"

"Millions?" asked Mrs. Shelton, smiling.

"Well, a lot. I'm going up front to look for Dad."

"Me, too," Diane said.

"I'll go with you," Grandpa Shelton told the twins. "I want to take Ben's picture."

Grandpa Shelton took his camera from the small shopping bag he had brought to the graduation. Then he hurried down the aisle with Donna and Diane.

Eric looked in the bag.

"Grandpa has something wrapped in silver paper."

Mrs. Shelton said, "That's a gift for Dad."

"Do you know what it is?"

Mrs. Shelton shook her head. She didn't know.

"Do you know how many graduates there are?" Eric asked.

Mrs. Shelton shook her head again.

"I don't know how many there are," Cam said, "but I know how to find out. We just have to count the number of names in the printed program."

Eric opened the graduation program and started to count.

Then he stopped.

"Did you already look at the program?" he asked Cam.

"Yes."

Eric laughed.

"Close your eyes and say, *'Click!'* Look at the pictures you have in your head of all the names on the program. Then tell me how many graduates there are."

Cam closed her eyes. She said, *"Click!"* Then, with her eyes still closed, she said, "There are six pages of names. Each page has four columns."

With her eyes still closed Cam counted the names in the first column.

"One, two, three . . . eighteen, nineteen, twenty."

Cam Jansen has a photographic memory. After she takes just one look at something, she remembers it perfectly. It's as if she has a mental camera and pictures in her head of everything she's seen.

Cam says, *"Click!"* whenever she wants to remember something. She says it's the sound her mental camera makes.

"Six pages of names with four columns on each page," Cam said. "That's twenty-four columns. There are twenty names in each column."

Cam opened her eyes.

"We just have to multiply twenty-four by twenty."

"I'll do that," Eric said. "I'm good at math."

Eric borrowed his mother's pen. He wrote the problem on the back of his program.

"Cam," Eric said. "There are four hundred and eighty graduates."

Cam's real name is Jennifer. But when people found out about her amazing memory they started calling her "The Camera." Soon "The Camera" was shortened to "Cam."

Meow!

"Hey, Mom," Harry said. "There's a cat at the graduation."

Harry held out a few animal crackers.

"Here, kitty. Have a giraffe. Have a monkey."

Meow!

"Hey, Mom," Harry said. "The cat ate the cookies."

A woman in a black cap and gown

stood on the platform. She tapped on the microphone.

Tap! Tap! Tap!

"Please be seated," she said. "We are about to begin."

Chapter Two

"That's Dr. Bette Guterman," Eric's mother whispered. "She's the president of the college."

The large crowd was suddenly quiet. Donna, Diane, and Grandpa Shelton hurried to their seats.

"We found Dad," Donna said. "He's sitting in the middle of the fourth row. We waved to him, and he waved back."

"Everyone please rise," Dr. Guterman said.

Thousands of people in the huge field stood.

Mrs. Shelton stood slowly. She didn't want to wake Howie.

"Stand straight," the woman sitting behind the Sheltons told her son. "Hold your hand over your heart."

Harry held his hand and his toy train over his heart.

"Hold your paw to your heart," Harry told the cat.

Dr. Guterman and the people at the graduation faced the flag of the United States. They recited the pledge of allegiance. Then they sang the national anthem.

Dr. Guterman asked everyone to be seated.

"What happens now?" Diane asked.

Grandpa looked at his program.

"A speech," Grandpa answered.

"And then what?" Diane asked.

"Another speech," Grandpa said, "and another, and another."

Diane complained, "No one told me I'd have to listen to so many speeches."

"You don't have to listen," her mother whispered. "You just have to sit quietly."

Diane and Donna sat quietly for a while. Then they played with Harry and the cat.

Cam and Eric turned and watched Donna, Diane, and Harry feed the cat animal crackers.

"It's almost over," Mrs. Shelton whispered to Cam and Eric. "The graduates are getting their diplomas."

One by one Dr. Guterman called out the names of the graduates in the order they were listed in the program. One by one the graduates stepped onto the platform. They received their diplomas. Then they returned to their seats.

"Yay, Jacob!" a few people sitting in front of the Sheltons called out.

A young man with short dark hair had just received his diploma. He held it up and smiled.

"Yay, Margery!" Harry and his mother called out.

A young woman just climbing onto the platform turned and bowed to the crowd.

Donna said, "I'm hungry."

"Soon we're going to a restaurant," Grandpa told her. "You'll have plenty to eat."

"Anne Sheldon," Dr. Guterman called.

"Nancy Sheller."

"Dad is next," Mrs. Shelton whispered.

Grandpa hurried down the aisle.

"Benjamin Shelton," Dr. Guterman called.

Eric told Cam, "Benjamin is Dad's real name. Ben is just what most people call him. It's his nickname."

Cam said, "I know about nicknames."

Mr. Shelton stepped onto the platform.

Cam stood. She looked straight at Eric's father. She blinked her eyes and said, *"Click!"*

Mrs. Shelton stood. She was holding baby Howie. Eric and the twins stood, too.

Dr. Guterman gave Mr. Shelton his diploma. He held it up and smiled.

"Yay!" Mrs. Shelton and Cam called out.

"Yay, Dad!" Eric and the twins called out.

Howie opened his eyes. He looked at his mother and smiled.

"Isaac Shulman," Dr. Guterman called.

Grandpa Shelton hurried back to his seat.

"Look," he said, and showed everyone the small screen on the back of his digital camera. "I took some great pictures of Ben."

"I took pictures, too," Cam said, "but I

took mine with my mental camera."

After all the graduates had received their diplomas, Dr. Guterman held up her hands. She wanted everyone to be quiet.

"What's happening now?" Diane asked.

"I don't know," her mother whispered. "There's nothing else listed on the program."

Everyone was quiet. They looked at Dr. Guterman and waited.

Dr. Guterman smiled. Then she announced, "Congratulations to the graduates!"

The graduates cheered. Many of them threw their caps into the air. The people in the audience cheered, too.

"Yay!" Donna and Diane called out.

They threw their programs into the air.

"That's it," Grandpa Shelton said. "When Ben gets here we'll all go to Green Stripes Restaurant to celebrate."

Donna and Diane picked up their programs.

The graduates walked down the center

aisle. When they reached their friends and families there were lots of hugs, kisses, and happy cheers.

Eric's father smiled and held up his diploma as he walked toward his family.

"Yay, Dad!" Eric called out.

Mrs. Shelton hugged her husband. Grandpa Shelton and all the children applauded.

"Grandpa has a surprise for you," Eric said.

"It's right in here," Grandpa said.

He held up a small shopping bag.

"Let me see," Diane said.

"It's wrapped in silver paper," Grandpa said. "No one sees what's inside until I give it to Ben at the restaurant."

Diane looked in the bag.

"Grandpa," Diane said. "There's nothing silver in here. All you have are toys, crackers, and apple juice."

Chapter Three

Grandpa opened the bag. He took out a small toy train.

"Is that the present you got for Dad?" Diane asked. "If he doesn't want it, I'll take it!"

Grandpa shook his head.

"This toy is not mine."

He looked in the bag and said, "None of the things in here are mine."

Eric said, "That train looks like the one Harry had. He sat behind us."

Grandpa looked under his chair. He looked under all the chairs in the row.

"Please," he said. "Help me find my bag. There's something very valuable in it."

"I know what's so valuable," Diane said. "It's the surprise you have for Dad."

The Sheltons and Cam looked under all the chairs in their row and the ones in the nearby rows, too.

"Look what I found," Diane said. "Lots of programs. When Donna and I get home we can have a pretend graduation. I'll be the president and make a really long speech."

"And I'll be a graduate," Donna said. "I'll get a *pildoma*."

"Diploma," her mother said.

"Grandpa," Diane said. "Maybe you took the bag with you when you went to take Dad's picture. Maybe the bag is all the way up front."

Grandpa shook his head and said, "No, I took the camera out of the bag when I walked to the front. Then I put it back."

"I'm going to look up front," Mr. Shelton said. "In a big crowd sometimes things get moved."

Cam and Eric went with him.

The cat followed them.

Grandpa, Mrs. Shelton, and the twins continued to look near their seats.

Cam, Eric, and Mr. Shelton walked through the crowd of people leaving the field.

"Look carefully at what everyone is carrying," Eric said. "Maybe someone has Grandpa's bag."

"Is it just a regular small brown shopping bag?" Mr. Shelton asked.

Cam closed her eyes. She said, "*Click!*"

Cam bumped into a tall man wearing a black cap and gown.

"Excuse me," the man said.

She bumped into the cat.

Meow!

Eric took Cam's hand.

"Yes," Cam said with her eyes still closed. "I'm looking at the picture I have in my head of Grandpa's shopping bag, and it's brown and not very big. It has two small brown rope handles."

Cam opened her eyes.

"I haven't seen anyone carrying a bag like that," Mr. Shelton said.

They looked under rows and rows of chairs near the platform, but they didn't find the bag.

"Let's go back," Mr. Shelton told Cam and Eric. "It's not here."

As they walked back to where Eric's family was sitting, they looked under all the rows of chairs.

When they got back, Mrs. Shelton was still holding Howie. He was sleeping. Grandpa was next to them. On the chair on the other side of Grandpa was the bag with the toys, animal crackers, and apple juice.

"We didn't find it," Mr. Shelton told Grandpa.

"This is terrible," Grandpa said. "The gift I had in there can't be replaced. And my camera with all my pictures of the graduation is also in there."

"Is the gift worth lots of money?" Donna asked.

"Yes. And it's been in the Shelton family for almost one hundred years."

"I think I know what happened," Donna said. "I think Harry took Grandpa's bag."

"That's it!" Diane said. "He took Grandpa's shopping bag by mistake."

"I think she's right," Mr. Shelton told his father.

"Yay!" Diane said. "We did it! Donna and I solved the mystery."

"You solved one mystery," Cam said, "but

22

Grandpa Shelton still doesn't have his bag. Maybe someone found it and gave it to the security people."

"Now there's another mystery to solve," Eric said. "We think Harry took Grandpa's bag, but where is Harry? We don't even know his last name. We have to find out who this Harry is and where he is. We have to get Grandpa's bag back."

Chapter Four

"What do we do now?" Eric asked.

"We do what Cam suggested," Mrs. Shelton said. "We tell the security people what happened. Maybe the boy didn't take Grandpa's bag, and someone found it. Maybe his mother realized it wasn't his bag and gave it to one of the guards."

Cam and the Sheltons went to the gate at one end of the field. A man and woman in green and yellow uniforms were sitting behind a table. Grandpa told them what happened. Eric showed them the bag they had—the wrong bag.

"It sounds like a simple mistake," one of the guards said. "Hopefully the woman and the little boy who took your bag will come back here with it."

Grandpa told the guards what was in his bag.

"My camera is digital. When you find it, look at the pictures and you'll know it's mine. Almost all of the ones I took today are of my son."

"That's me," Mr. Shelton told the guards.

"Give us your cell phone number," the first guard said. "We'll call you if the woman and her son come back."

"What about this bag?" Grandpa asked.

"Leave it here."

Grandpa left the bag on the table. Then he wrote his cell phone number on a small piece of paper. The guards gave him a card with their number.

"I'm Janet Jones," the woman guard said.

"I'm Paul Cogan," the other guard said. "I hope we find your things."

Cam and the Sheltons walked away from the table.

"What do we do now?" Grandpa Shelton asked.

"Dad is a college graduate," Mrs. Shelton said. "We will still go to Green Stripes Restaurant and celebrate. We can walk there. It's just a few blocks away."

Mr. Shelton held Donna and Diane's hands. Mrs. Shelton put Howie in a stroller.

The cat followed them as they walked through two large stone columns at the entrance to the campus.

Mr. Shelton stopped.

"Good-bye," he said to the columns and to the college. "And thank you."

He started walking toward the restaurant.

Mrs. Shelton stood by the entrance to the college.

"Aren't you forgetting something?" she asked.

Mr. Shelton looked at Donna and Diane. He looked at Howie in his stroller. He looked at Grandpa, Eric, and Cam.

"No," he said. "Everyone is here."

"What about your cap and gown?" Mrs. Shelton asked.

"Oh! Am I still wearing them?"

Mr. Shelton took off his cap and gown. He put them in a zippered bag strapped to the back of Howie's stroller. Then the Sheltons and Cam walked to Green Stripes Restaurant.

"Look at the line," Grandpa Shelton said.

"I called. They're expecting us," Eric's

mother told him. "We shouldn't have to wait."

Mrs. Shelton went to the front of the line. She spoke to a woman in a green striped dress. Mrs. Shelton waved to her family and Cam.

Eric told the cat, "You can't come in with us."

Meow!

The cat sat on the sidewalk. She watched as Cam and the Sheltons followed the woman in the green striped dress into the restaurant.

"Wow!" Cam whispered to Eric. "This is a fancy place."

The tables were covered with green striped cloths. The waiters wore green striped bow ties and jackets. The woman in the green striped dress led the Sheltons and Cam past lots of tables and lots of people. She led them down a few steps to the lower level of the restaurant.

"Please be seated," she said when they

came to a long empty table. "Your waiter will be here soon."

She brought a high chair for Howie.

"Look at the walls. Look at all the pictures," Eric whispered. "This place is like a museum."

Cam and Eric sat on one side of the table. Grandpa sat next to Cam.

A tall man in a green striped jacket came to the table. He gave everyone a menu.

"My name is Roger," the waiter told everyone at the table. "Our brunch specials today

are orange-glazed tuna and old country French toast."

"I don't want old toast," Diane said. "I want it to be new."

Roger smiled.

"The French toast is fresh," he said. "It's the recipe that's old."

The children each ordered French toast. Eric's parents and grandfather ordered the fish.

"It's not just my surprise for Ben that's gone," Grandpa said while he waited for his meal. "All the pictures I took are gone, too."

"I have a camera," Eric's mom said. "Ben still has his cap and gown. When we get home we'll take new pictures."

"We could do that," Grandpa said sadly, "but it won't be the same. I took a picture of Ben getting his diploma. He had such a great big smile."

"Look at all the people here," Eric whispered to Cam. "I bet lots of them were at the graduation."

Cam looked around.

"I think you're right," she said.

Eric whispered, "Maybe Harry and his mother are here. Maybe he doesn't even know he took the wrong bag."

"Let's look," Cam said.

Chapter Five

Eric told his mother that he and Cam were going to take a walk through the restaurant.

"Don't bother anyone," his mother said. "And don't get in the way of any of the waiters."

Cam and Eric looked at the people in the lower level of the restaurant. Several children were sitting at a table in the corner.

"Look," Eric whispered. "Look at the boy in the blue shirt. He looks like Harry."

Cam shook her head and whispered, "That's not him."

"Are you sure?"

Cam closed her eyes and said, *"Click!"*

Cam told Eric, "Harry had on a white shirt, dark blue pants, and black shoes. His hair was combed back."

Cam opened her eyes. She pointed to the boy in the restaurant and whispered, "That's not him."

Eric said, "You never clicked for the college

guards. You never told them what Harry and his mother look like."

"Excuse me," a waiter said. He held a tray of dirty dishes high over his head as he walked past.

Eric said, "Let's ask Grandpa to call the guards."

Cam and Eric went back to their table. Roger had brought them a basket of rolls and pats of butter.

"These rolls are hot," Diane said. "Watch this."

She broke open a roll and dropped in a pat of butter.

"It's melting!"

Eric's grandfather called the guards. He asked if they had found his bag. Grandpa listened for a moment and then sadly shook his head. He gave his cell phone to Cam. She closed her eyes and said, *"Click."* Then she described Harry and his mother to the guards.

"Now let's check upstairs for him," Eric said to Cam.

Cam and Eric walked to the upper level of the restaurant.

"This is a strange mystery," Cam told Eric as they climbed the steps. "We know who has Grandpa's things. We just don't know how to find him."

Cam and Eric walked from one table to the next. There were lots of children in the restaurant, but none of them was the boy who sat behind them at the graduation.

"Those are the doors to the kitchen," Cam said. "We've been through the whole restaurant. Harry isn't here."

Eric walked to a quiet corner near the kitchen doors.

A waiter carrying a tray of dirty dishes walked past. He pushed open a swinging door and went into the kitchen.

"What do we do now?" Eric asked.

Cam shook her head. She didn't know.

The other kitchen door swung open. A waiter walked out with a tray covered with plates of French toast.

"That's our waiter," Cam said. "That's Roger."

Another waiter followed Roger with three plates of tuna.

"They're carrying French toast and fish," Eric said. "That's our food. Let's go."

Chapter Six

"Excuse me," Eric said as he hurried past the two waiters.

"Excuse me," Cam said.

They went down the few steps to the lower level of the restaurant and to their table. Mrs. Shelton was holding and feeding Howie.

"Our meals are coming," Eric said.

The two waiters came to the table with French toast and three tunas.

"Yummy," Diane said as she held a small pitcher over her toast and covered it with syrup.

The twins got syrup on their faces and clothes.

When they were done eating, Roger brought them dessert menus.

Eric's parents and Grandpa Shelton ordered tea and cookies. Cam, Eric, and Donna asked for ice cream.

"I don't want ice cream," Diane said. "I want a big piece of chocolate cake."

After Roger left, Diane told her sister, "The chocolate cake has gooey chocolate cream inside. That's what my friend Carol told me. She's been here lots of times."

Grandpa stood.

"This is when I planned to give you a special gift. It was my grandfather's gold watch. The watch was his graduation gift to my father. It was my father's graduation gift to me. Ben, it was going to be my gift to you. I don't have the watch to give, but I'm still very proud of you."

"Thank you, Dad," Mr. Shelton said, and hugged his father.

Roger brought the desserts.

"Yummy," Donna said after she tasted her ice cream.

Diane poked her cake with her fork.

"Hey, there's no chocolate cream."

Roger took a small pad from the pocket in his apron.

"You asked for chocolate cake," Roger said. "That's chocolate cake."

"Where's the gooey cream?"

"There's no cream in the regular chocolate cake," Roger told Diane. "It's in the chocolate *mousse* cake."

"Moose! My friend didn't say there's a moose with horns in the cake. She said it had cream."

"It's a different kind of moose," Roger explained. "It's not spelled the same."

He smiled. "I'll change it for the one with cream."

Roger took Diane's cake away.

"Names and spelling are important when you order food in a restaurant," Mrs. Shelton told Diane.

Cam put down her spoon.

"Did you hear that?" she whispered to Eric. "Names are important."

"Of course names are important. My name, Eric, means 'mighty one.'"

"A name can solve this mystery. A name

can help us get back Grandpa's things," Cam said. "I remember exactly what Harry and his mother look like. I just have to remember the name they called out when Dr. Guterman gave out the diplomas."

Chapter Seven

Roger brought Diane a slice of chocolate mousse cake.

Diane stuck her finger in the cream and tasted it.

"Yummy," she said.

"Please, thank Roger," her mother told Diane. "And please, eat with a fork."

"Thank you," Diane said to Roger.

Diane broke off a large piece of the cake with her fork.

"*'Choo! Choo!* All aboard!'" Eric said. "That's what the boy called out."

"He cheered for someone when she went

to get her diploma," Cam said. "He yelled, 'Yay, Margery!'"

"Eat your ice cream before it melts," Mrs. Shelton told Cam and Eric.

They each ate some ice cream.

"We have to find a woman named Margery who just graduated from your dad's college," Cam said. "She'll know who the boy is. Then we'll find Grandpa's bag. Donna and Diane can tell us Margery's full name."

Roger cleared away their dessert dishes.

"My sisters can't help us," Eric said. "They don't know the names of the graduates."

"They have lots of printed lists of their names," Cam said. "The names of all the graduates are in the programs."

"Diane," Eric asked. "Can I see one of the graduation programs?"

Diane took a handful of crumpled papers from her pocket. She gave them to Eric.

"I have more," she said.

Diane took another handful of papers from her other pocket and gave those to Eric, too.

"You have to give them back when you're done," she said. "When we get home, Donna and I will need them to play our graduation game."

Eric uncrumpled two of the programs. He gave one to Cam.

"I'm looking for first names that begin with 'M,'" Eric said as he ran his finger down the list of names.

"Michael . . . Martin . . . Margaret . . .

Another Michael . . . Here's a Margery. Margery Dubin."

"I found one, too," Cam said. "Margery Miller."

"Is that it?" Eric asked. "Are there just two graduates named Margery?"

"That's it. Now we have to call the guards at the college. Maybe they can find the two Margerys."

Roger came to the table with a small plate. On it was the bill for the meal.

"I'll take that," Mrs. Shelton said.

"No, I'll pay," Grandpa told her. "Ben is my son, and this celebration is my treat."

"Grandpa," Mrs. Shelton said, and smiled. "Can we share?"

Grandpa nodded.

Eric's mother and grandfather paid the bill. Then Eric asked his grandfather to call the guards. He told him that Margery Dubin or Margery Miller could help them find his bag.

Grandpa spoke to the guards. Then he closed his cell phone.

"They'll check with the college office to find the two women's telephone numbers. If they can, they'll call them, and if one has my bag they'll ask her to bring it to the college."

"What do we do now?" Eric asked.

"We walk back to our car," Grandpa said.

"Look at the twins," Mrs. Shelton said. "We're not going anywhere with them looking like that."

Diane had chocolate cream on her face, hands, and dress. Donna had melted ice

cream on her face. They were both sticky with syrup.

Everyone waited while Diane and Donna went to the bathroom and washed. Then Cam and the Sheltons left Green Stripes.

Howie started to cry. Mrs. Shelton took him from his stroller and held him.

Meow!

"The cat waited for us!" Eric said. He bent down and petted the cat. "Cam said names are important, so we should give her a name."

Diane said, "Let's call her Mrs. Talbot. She was my kindergarten teacher."

"No," Eric said. "Let's call her CC. That's short for College Cat."

"CC," Donna said. "I like that."

"Cam," Eric said. "Your great photographic memory solved another mystery."

"No," Cam said, and shook her head. "I didn't look at pictures in my head to find Grandpa's bag. I remembered something Harry said."

"Right now nothing has been solved," Grandpa said. "I still don't have Ben's gift or my camera."

They all walked for a while. They came to the two stone columns at the entrance gates to the college, and Mrs. Shelton stopped.

"I forgot where I parked my car."

Cam smiled. She closed her eyes and said, *"Click!"*

"Your car is near the corner of Seventh and Franklin," Cam said with her eyes still closed. "It's between a red SUV and a motorcycle."

Cam opened her eyes.

Grandpa took a paper from his pocket and said, "I know where I parked my car. I wrote it down."

"Wait," Eric said. "Before we go home, let's talk to the guards."

"You can stay with Grandpa," Mrs. Shelton said. "Howie was good for a long time, but now he's restless. I need to get him home."

The twins went with Mrs. Shelton.

Grandpa, Mr. Shelton, Cam, and Eric walked back onto the college campus.

"There they are," Eric said. "They're still sitting by the table."

Eric waved to them.

The guard named Paul Cogan stood.

"I have good news!" he shouted.

Chapter Eight

"I was just going to call you. We spoke to both Margerys," the other guard, Janet Jones, told Grandpa. "Margery Miller has your things."

"She said she was really glad we called," the other guard added. "Her little brother was very upset. He wants his toy trains. Luckily, she lives nearby. She'll be here soon."

"I was also very upset," Grandpa said. "I have important things in that bag."

Mr. Shelton, Grandpa, Cam, Eric, and CC waited by the two stone columns. Lots of cars went past. Then one of them stopped. Two women and Harry got out. The older of

the two women was carrying a small brown
shopping bag.

Harry ran to CC.

"Hello, cat. I missed you."

"I'm so sorry," the woman said, giving
the bag to Grandpa. "My son took this by
mistake."

The two bags looked exactly alike.

"It was an easy mistake to make. This is yours," Grandpa said.

Grandpa gave the woman the other bag. The woman gave it to Harry. Then she thanked Janet and Grandpa.

"Hey, cat," Harry said. "We brought you something to eat."

Margery opened a can of cat food and put it on the ground. CC ran to it.

Margery told the Sheltons, "She lives under the science center steps. We all feed her."

Grandpa took out a small silver-wrapped package from his bag. He gave it to Eric's father.

"Open it," Grandpa said.

Mr. Shelton unwrapped the package. He took out a gold watch and showed it to Cam and Eric.

"Put it on," Grandpa said.

Mr. Shelton put the watch on.

"Thank you so much," Mr. Shelton said

to Grandpa. "This was once your old watch.
Now it's my new watch. I love it."

"What time is it?" Grandpa asked.

Mr. Shelton looked at his watch, and
Grandpa took his picture.

"It's almost two o'clock," Mr. Shelton said.

Grandpa laughed.

"I know what time it is. I just wanted a picture of you looking at the watch. I'm going
to make an album of your graduation."

"Smile," Grandpa told Cam and Eric. "I want a picture in the album of my grandson and his very best friend."

Cam and Eric smiled, and Grandpa Shelton took their picture.

"Thank you for solving the mystery," Grandpa said to Cam and Eric. "I didn't think I'd ever get my things back."

Then Grandpa thanked the two guards and took their pictures.

"It's for my album," Grandpa told the guards.

"I already have an album," Cam told the Sheltons. "It's up here in my head. I have lots of pictures of my very best friend and his very nice family."

A Cam Jansen Memory Game

Take another look at the picture opposite page 1. Study it. Blink your eyes and say, *"Click!"* Then turn back here and answer the questions at the bottom of the page. Please, first study the picture, *then* look at the questions.

1. How many people are standing on the stage? How many are sitting on the stage?

2. Is there a flag in the picture?

3. Is Eric sitting next to his twin sisters?

4. Is Grandpa wearing a hat?

5. What's written on the sign above the stage?

6. Are baby Howie's eyes open or closed?